D1097380

# THE
# ANIMAL
# SONG

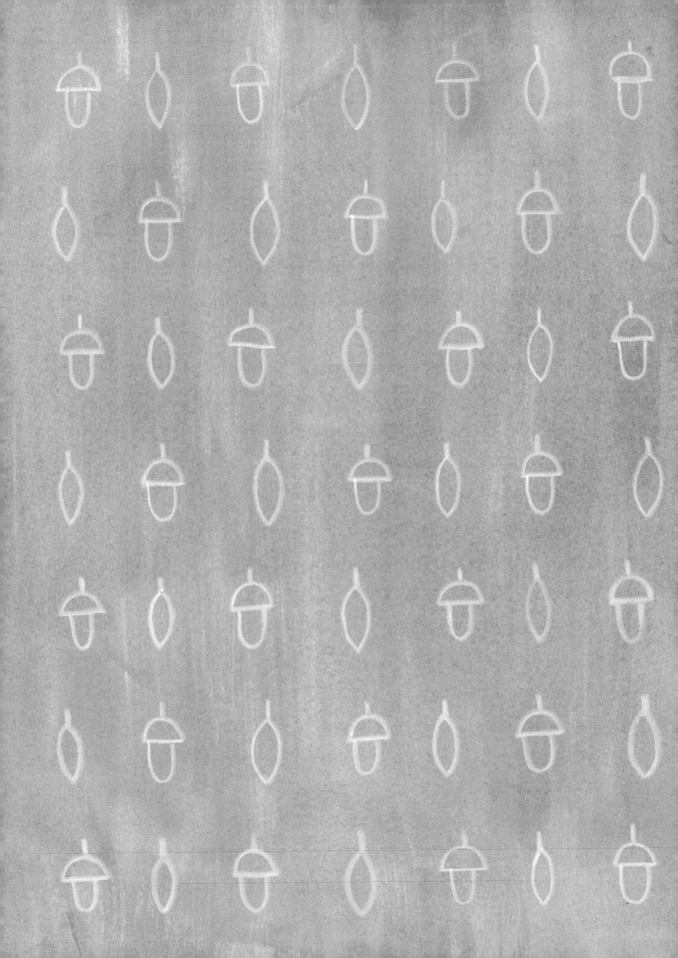

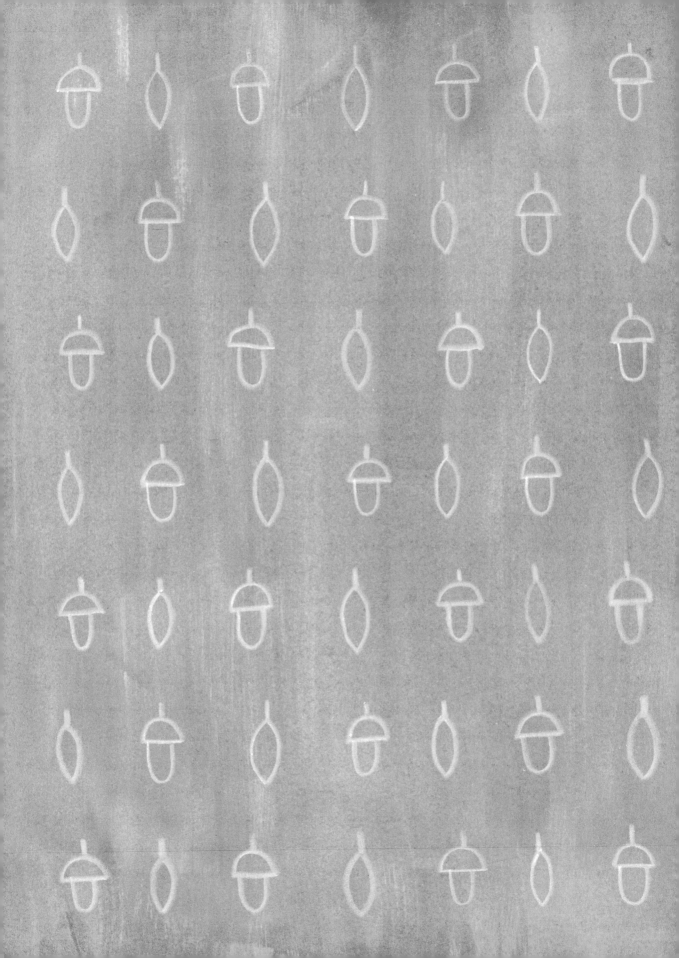

This book belongs to:

## For Hannah

Copyright © 2023 by Jonty Howley
All rights reserved. Published in the United States by Random House Studio,
an imprint of Random House Children's Books, a division of Penguin Random House LLC, New York.
Random House Studio and the colophon are registered trademarks of Penguin Random House LLC.
Visit us on the Web! rhcbooks.com
Educators and librarians, for a variety of teaching tools, visit us at RHTeachersLibrarians.com
Library of Congress Cataloging-in-Publication Data is available upon request.
ISBN 978-0-593-38146-5 (trade) — ISBN 978-0-593-38147-2 (library binding) — ISBN 978-0-593-38148-9 (ebook)
ISBN 978-0-593-81242-6 (proprietary)

The text of this book is set in 22-point Futura Now Headline.
The illustrations were rendered in gouache, crayon, and colored pencil, and edited digitally.
Book design by Elizabeth Tardiff

MANUFACTURED IN CHINA
10 9 8 7 6 5 4 3 2 1
First Edition

Random House Children's Books supports the First Amendment and celebrates the right to read.

Penguin Random House LLC supports copyright. Copyright fuels creativity, encourages diverse voices, promotes free speech,
and creates a vibrant culture. Thank you for buying an authorized edition of this book and for complying with
copyright laws by not reproducing, scanning, or distributing any part in any form without permission.
You are supporting writers and allowing Penguin Random House to publish books for every reader.

This Imagination Library edition is published by Random House Children's Books, a division of Penguin Random House LLC, exclusively for
Dolly Parton's Imagination Library, a not-for-profit program dedicated to inspire a love of reading and learning, sponsored in part by
The Dollywood Foundation. Penguin Random House's trade editions of this work are available where all books are sold.

# THE
# ANIMAL
# SONG

## JONTY HOWLEY

RANDOM HOUSE STUDIO ⌂ NEW YORK

**Snap** went the croc
on the little snare drum.

**Poom-poom,**

the big brown bear
thumped with his thumb.

**Jingle-jangle,**

strummed the weasel,
all steady and strong.

Snap-poom-jingle-jangle
went the animal song.

Everyone in the wood loved the animal song,
and they sang it out loud all summer long.

But when winter came, they all said,
"Shhh, now, please, we want to go to bed!"

But the band wasn't tired
and their rhythm was strong.
So snap-poom-jingle-jangle
went the animal song.

The band played for a squirrel
in the knot of a tree.
"Shhh, now, please, it's bedtime for me."

But the band wasn't sleepy.
"I guess we'll move along."

And snap-poom-jingle-jangle
went the animal song.

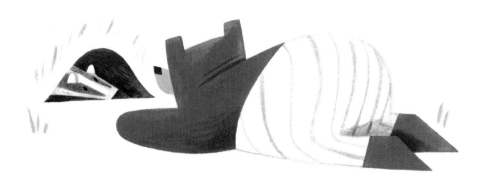

They tried
the badger

and the bat,

the hedgehog
and the sow,

but they all said,
"Shhh! It's time for
bed now."

"Well, that's everyone,"
said the bear with a frown.
"Everyone?" said the rat.
"Have you tried the town?"

"Of course!"                    "The town!"

"They say it never sleeps!"
And with a snap-poom-jangle
they were back on their feet.

They marched through the woods,
the fields, and the brook.

They really didn't care how long it took.

Soon they were playing
their song in full swing,
and like the rat said,
the town joined in.

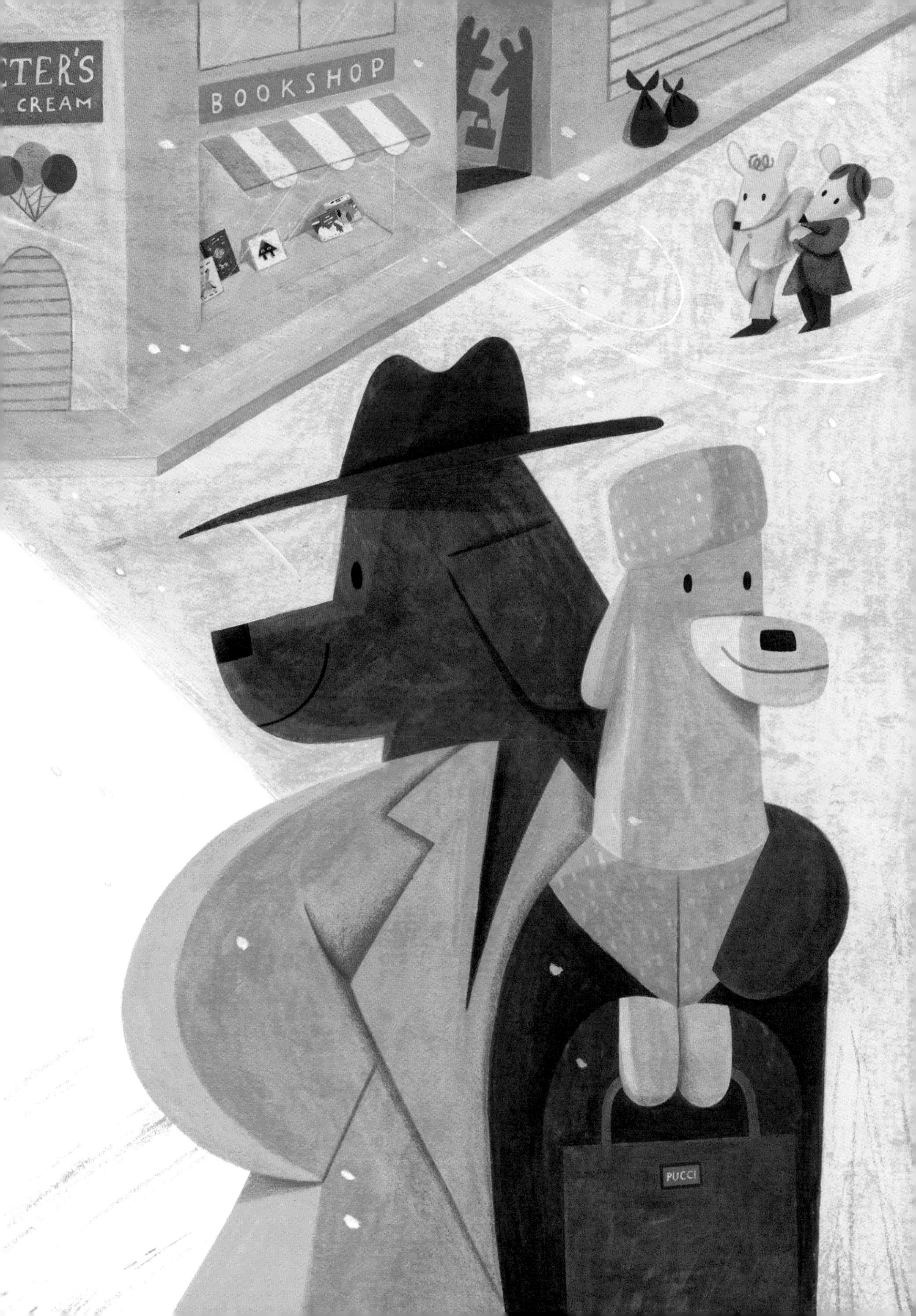

CTER'S
CREAM
BOOKSHOP
PUCCI

But night
after night,

day after day,

there was always someone there,
asking them to play.

By winter's end, it wasn't fun anymore.
The band was exhausted. *"My paws are sore."*

So quietly now, they set off, slow,
back home through the fields and the
melting snow. . . .

Soon the woods woke up and gathered to sing
the animal song as they did every spring.
They waited and waited, but the band never came,

"Shhh, now, please," said the bear with a yawn.

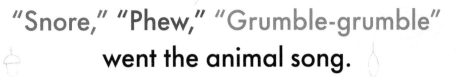

"Snore," "Phew," "Grumble-grumble"
went the animal song.

# The Animal Song

## Jonty Howley

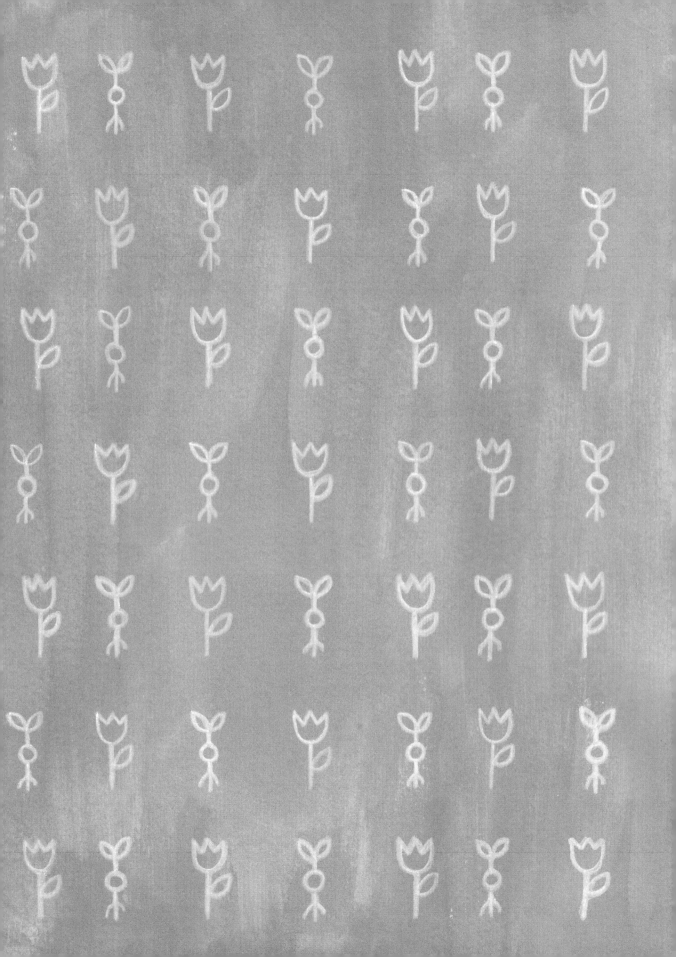

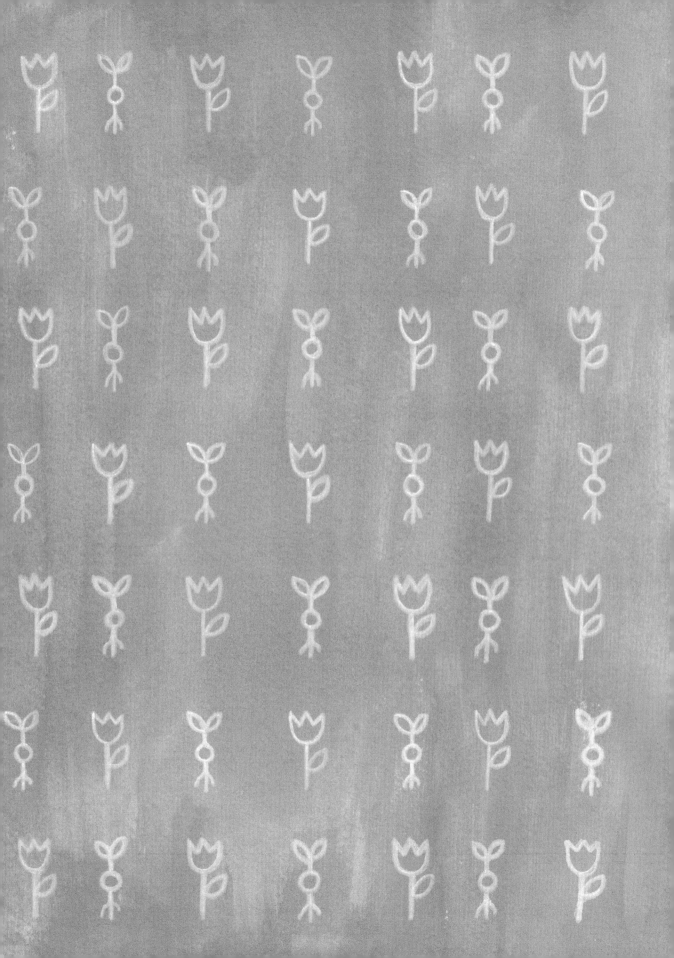